MW00943623

©2019 by Katie Lantz

Prologue

Eleanor Beachy took in a deep breath of the chilly morning air and pulled her shawl a little bit tighter against her body. It felt like the early January wind was biting even colder than usual this morning, and snowflakes were starting to spit from the sky.

Making her way down the sidewalk in her small hometown, Eleanor smiled when she heard the sound of the nearby train rumbling down the track. Turning on her heel, Eleanor watched the train in the distance and thought about all the times that she and her friends had giggled and made plans together when they were younger. Eleanor could remember the sleepovers when the girls would whisper plans to gather enough money to ride to a big city and see what the Englischer world had to offer.

As part of the Amish community, Eleanor and her friends knew exactly what was expected of them in life. They were supposed to grow up, get married, and then raise children in the faith. However, between growing up and getting married, there were the teenage years … the years of the rumspringa when Amish boys and girls were allowed to run around and sow their wild oats, enjoying the opportunity to experience the Englischer world before they were baptized and became members of the Amish church.

Shaking her head to herself, Eleanor had to smile thinking about it. At eighteen years old, she was drawing near the end of her own rumspringa. While Eleanor had done some wilder things, such as listen to radio music, and even watched some programs on television at a house that she cleaned, she had gone through her teen years without straying far from her conservative faith roots.

While Eleanor didn't regret her decision to stay close to her home and cling to her faith, there was something that seemed horribly depressing about seeing her friends getting married … and realizing that marriage soon awaited her.

Making her way through the small Indiana town, Eleanor bit down on her lip as she considered life and the way that things had turned out.

Each morning, she got up early and headed into town to help at her father's candle shop. Sometimes she rode by buggy, but most often, she would walk the short distance by foot. There was something about walking that made Eleanor feel better about life in general. While it could be lonely and gave her almost too much time to think, overall, she felt reenergized by the world around her.

As the train disappeared from sight, Eleanor took in a deep breath and continued down the sidewalk. Noticing someone she recognized, she waved at a passing car. Working in the candle shop, Eleanor had gained many friends within the Englischer and Amish communities. Everyone in the area loved her father's scented candles and stopped by frequently to make purchases.

Out of the corner of her eye, Eleanor could see something floating across the pavement in front of her. Squinting, Eleanor looked closer and could see that it was a twenty-dollar bill. Raising her eyebrows,

Eleanor instantly wondered who might have lost the money. She wasn't sure, but she was going to do whatever she could to get it. She knew how hard money could be to come by, and she was determined that she would save the money and return it to its rightful owner.

Taking one big leap after another across the sidewalk, she reached a hand out and grabbed for the money. To her surprise, her fingers brushed against someone else's as she clasped the bill.

Looking up in shock, Eleanor found herself staring directly into the eyes of a stranger. The most handsome stranger she had ever seen before. Dressed in Amish clothing, the young man had a shock of brown hair hidden beneath his black felt hat. When his eyes met Eleanor's, she thought she might get lost in the depths of their darkness.

Pulling herself into a standing position, Eleanor held tightly to the bill and found herself struggling to gain her composure.

"Hello," Eleanor said with a smile, hoping that her voice didn't reveal how nervous she found herself. "Here … would this be yours?"

The young man smiled in return, his face crinkling as he grinned and reached out a hand. "It sure is. Thanks for helping me catch it!"

"You're welcome," Eleanor replied as she handed him the money. "I'm Eleanor."

"Danke again. I'm Simon Nissley." As the young man reached for the bill, he grabbed onto Eleanor's hand, giving it a tender shake.

There was something about the feel of his skin against hers that made Eleanor feel instantly warm and seemed to make her skin almost tingle. As she studied his face, she was almost certain that she could see his cheeks start to flush, as if he could feel it as well.

Regaining her good sense, Eleanor managed to pull her hand away, leaving Simon to shove his down in his pockets.

"I'm here visiting my aunt and uncle," he explained as he looked down at the sidewalk. "Lavern and Joyce. They own the woodworking shop up the street."

Nodding her head, Eleanor recognized the names. She knew Lavern and Joyce well; they had made the hand-carved hope chest that sat at the foot of her bed. For so many years, she had been putting special handmade items in the chest, looking forward to the day when she would have a husband of her own.

Eleanor realized that she was staring at Simon much longer than was truly proper, but despite her best intentions, she couldn't seem to pull her eyes away from him. He was so handsome, and at the same time, so strangely familiar. Surely, if she had seen him in the past, she would have remembered those enchanting eyes.

"Simon Nissley," she repeated the name again, saying it almost under her breath, searching her memory for any time that she might have met him before.

"Eleanor!" A loud voice pulled Eleanor from her thoughts. Looking away from Simon, she could see her boyfriend, Abe Miller, marching toward her.

Forcing herself to wave at her boyfriend, Eleanor tried to push aside the strange feelings that she had for the man in front of her.

"Eleanor," Abe repeated as he hurried to her side and reached out to take her arm in his own. "Eleanor, what is taking you so long? You know I've been waiting at the corner for at least ten minutes. If you want me to walk you part of the way to work, you've got to be more punctual."

That was Abe. In the two years that he and Eleanor had been dating, Eleanor had come to learn that he was a stickler for punctuality and doing things perfectly. He could certainly be a challenge to get along with at times, often going so far that Eleanor almost considered him mean, but he was her boyfriend and the only one that she had ever had.

"Come, Eleanor," Abe persisted as he began to practically drag her down the sidewalk. "We don't want you to be late for work."

Turning her head to glance back at Simon, Eleanor forced a smile and called out, "Goodbye, Simon. It was nice meeting you!"

Chapter One

Simon Nissley stood on the sidewalk and felt practically frozen in place. He watched as his newfound acquaintance, Eleanor, was dragged away by a strange Amish man who seemed to have appeared out of thin air.

Swallowing hard, Simon tried to push aside the torrent of emotions that seemed to assail him. He found himself feeling almost protective of Eleanor as if she belonged to him rather than the young man who had taken her by the arm and rushed her off to work.

Shaking his head, Simon gritted his teeth together and turned to head back toward his uncle's woodworking shop.

Who was that beautiful young woman? There had been something about her that had been so familiar and yet, at the same time, so mysterious. Simon could have almost promised that he had known her in his past, and yet he was certain that he wouldn't have forgotten her if they had met before.

Shaking his head to himself, Simon crossed his arms against his chest, trying to block the chilly air. Reaching Uncle Lavern's shop, Simon pushed the swinging glass door open and stepped inside. As soon as he stepped into the building, he was overwhelmed by the smell of freshly cut wood and the warmth from the coal stove.

Smiling to himself, Simon closed his eyes and breathed in deeply, allowing himself to get momentarily lost in the familiar scent.

"Ya all right, Simon?" The voice of his Aunt Joyce brought Simon from his thoughts and put an instant blush on his cheeks, making him as embarrassed as if he had actually been caught doing something he shouldn't.

Nodding his head ever so slowly, Simon pulled off the hand-knitted blue scarf that he had wrapped around his neck and hung it on a nail by the door along with his black felt hat.

"Jah, Joyce," Simon replied as he hurried to grab some sandpaper and start working on finishing up a table. "I'm fine. I guess I was just enjoying the smell of the shop."

Shaking her head to herself, Joyce smiled, dimples appearing all over her chubby cheeks. At forty-five years old, Joyce was not a young woman; however, she had an infectious way about her that made her seem nearer to Simon's own age.

Aunt Joyce and Uncle Lavern had always been some of Simon's favorite relatives. From the time that he was a little boy, he had always looked forward to the summers that he was able to travel from his home in Lancaster County, Pennsylvania, to Indiana to stay with his beloved relatives. While Simon had twelve brothers and sisters at home, when he went to Aunt Joyce's house, he was the only child. He had soaked up the visits as long as possible …

Thinking over those long-gone days, Simon felt a familiar lump rise in his throat. When Simon was about eleven years old, his father had determined that he enjoyed his visits to Indiana far too much and had put a stop to them. But Simon had vowed to himself that, no matter what his father said, he would eventually return to Indiana and put down roots.

Glancing across the room at Aunt Joyce, Simon considered his plans once again. His aunt and uncle believed that he was just there for a long visit, but Simon honestly hoped that it could turn into something permanent. He had always known that his heart was at home in Indiana, and he was ready to make sure that he spent the rest of his life here.

"How was your trip to the hardware store?" Uncle Lavern called out the back of the shop. "Did you get those nails that I needed?"

Simon had to laugh to himself as he remembered the small package of nails that was still buried away in his black coat pocket. Hurriedly, Simon took it to his uncle. It seemed so silly that he had forgotten to give his uncle the nails that he had been sent to fetch.

"Here." Simon pulled out the twenty-dollar bill, "There's your change. In my clumsiness, I almost lost it. You can thank a young woman for helping me catch it."

Lavern didn't say anything; instead, he just nodded his head, obviously distracted by the job in front of him. As one of the best woodworking shops in the county, Lavern had large work orders to keep up with. Most days, he had to work overtime, and often, Joyce had to join him. With no children of their own, keeping up with the orders was almost more than they could do by themselves.

They might be happy to know that I want to stay, Simon thought to himself as he looked over the wooden table that his uncle was polishing. Surely the idea of having an extra pair of hands around the shop would seem like a blessing to the couple.

"Just put the money there," Uncle Lavern instructed him, gesturing.

Setting the money and the nails on a nearby counter, Simon found himself almost hating to put aside his only tie to the beautiful young Amish woman he had encountered on the sidewalk. She had said that her name was Eleanor. Why did that sound so familiar? Now, Simon was kicking himself for not asking her for her last name and more details about her life.

For a moment, Simon considered asking Uncle Lavern exactly who Eleanor was; however, he forced himself to remain silent. For some reason, the idea of even mentioning the pretty young woman made him feel like blushing. No, Simon wouldn't mention her right now. Instead, he would focus on the work ahead of him and ask about her later.

Chapter Two

"Here you go!" Eleanor announced with a smile as she passed the shopping bag full of candles toward the Englisch customer, Mrs. Banks. "I hope you enjoy these candles. My dad made them to smell like butterscotch candy and maple butter … just like you were asking about."

The middle-aged woman smiled in return as she picked up the merchandise. "Thank you so much. Tell your father how much I appreciate his hard work. I always love to burn his candles in my house, and my friends all talk about how good they make my house smell."

Eleanor nodded her head. Even though she got constant compliments about her father's candles, she always appreciated hearing stories about the ways that they impacted the lives of others. Mrs. Banks was a long-time customer who came to the shop for all of her candle needs.

Watching her walk out of the shop, Eleanor found her eyes traveling to the window as she subconsciously searched the street.

"What are you searching for, you silly girl?" Eleanor asked out loud into the stillness of the shop.

Of course, she knew exactly what she was searching for—another glimpse of the handsome young man whom she had met that morning on the sidewalk.

"Simon Nissley," Eleanor repeated the name. Why did it sound so familiar?

Gritting her teeth together, Eleanor considered the way that Abe had acted after he'd seen her talking with Simon. He had been so angry! Even now, Eleanor could feel the way that his hand had clasped around her arm. He had held her tightly—almost as if she was his possession.

Abe had no right to be that upset over a chance encounter with a stranger! But, when Eleanor thought about the thrill that had run down her arm when she'd touched hands with Simon, she realized that her boyfriend might honestly have had a reason to be upset. She could only hope that her beau hadn't been able to see the feelings that she had suddenly experienced toward Simon.

"You're a fool, Eleanor!" she scolded herself as she crossed the room and began organizing candles on a shelf. "It's not like you to be knocked off-kilter by a handsome face!"

In Eleanor's eighteen years, she had never considered herself to be a giggly, silly girl. In fact, she was pretty levelheaded as a general rule. Eleanor wasn't one to start getting all emotional over a man she didn't even know.

Eleanor had Abe. No, he might not be perfect, but he was perfect for her. They had been together for two years now and, while Eleanor did have occasional doubts about her boyfriend, she had to push them aside. Abe Miller was the man for her, and she had to accept that.

She didn't have time to think about Simon Nissley. No, she needed to be more focused on building a life with Abe.

***

Sitting down in front of the rock fireplace in his uncle's home, Simon soaked in the warmth of the burning embers that were in front of him. There was something about this place that always seemed so peaceful and happy. At his side, Uncle Lavern was reading a magazine while Aunt Joyce darned a black sock, her rocking chair squeaking as she moved back and forth.

"How long do you get to stay this time?" Aunt Joyce asked Simon, her voice breaking the silence in the room.

Sucking in a deep breath, Simon tried to decide how much he should admit to his aunt.

"Well," he began slowly as he watched a log crackle in the fireplace, "I'm not quite sure yet … I'd like for it to be a while if you all will keep me."

Uncle Lavern laughed deeply as he turned a page in his magazine and nodded his head. "Ach, we'll let you stay for as long as you can. You always have a home here."

This announcement gave Simon the courage he needed to push forward and ask his next question. "Do you really mean that? Always?"

Aunt Joyce stopped rocking and, when Simon snuck a glance in her direction, he could see that she was staring at him intently.

"What do you mean, Simon?" she asked, her brow knitting in confusion.

Taking in a deep breath, Simon admitted, "Well, I'm not sure yet … but I'd definitely like to stay for a while. If I could, I might like to … well, move here permanently."

For a moment, it seemed like Simon's aunt and uncle were frozen in place, their jaws both dropped and their eyes large.

"Do you really mean it?" Aunt Joyce exclaimed when she finally found her voice. "Do you really think you might want to put down roots here?"

Simon nodded his head, his eyes starting to fill with tears when he realized that his aunt was happy with his announcement. He had been holding his breath ever since he'd arrived in Indiana, almost afraid of what he might do if they told him that he wasn't welcome for more than a few days.

As a young man, Simon didn't have much money. If he wanted to make a new life in Indiana, he would need the support of his uncle and aunt to help him get his feet under him. While Simon was happy to work for everything he hoped to have, he needed a place to stay until he could build a house of his own.

"Boy, you couldn't have said anything to make me much happier!" Uncle Lavern threw in. "Since Joyce and I have no children … well, you've certainly been the closest thing that we've ever had to a son."

Joyce's face was beaming as she announced, "Yes, we need you here, Simon! You can help in the shop … and you can live here with us until you get married …"

Holding up a hand, Simon hurried to stop her before she let her imagination run totally wild. "Aunt Joyce, don't start putting the cart before the horse on this one. I'm just thinking about staying. I haven't actually made up my mind yet! And, as far as getting married goes, well, I figure I'm about as close to an old bachelor as anyone I know. Most of the Amish girls my age are already married … I'm probably not the marrying type, anyway."

Chuckling to herself, Joyce replied, "Well, you might feel that way now, but your mind might change once you meet a few of the young women around here. Seems to me that, only a few years ago, you were pretty sweet on one of the girls around here."

Simon felt his face start to blush when he considered his encounter with Eleanor earlier that morning. Before he could stop himself, he blurted out, "Well, I did meet a young woman this morning … but she had a boyfriend with her. She said her name was

Eleanor. Do you know who she might be?" Aunt Joyce threw her sock aside and leaned forward in her chair, her eyes sparkling as she exclaimed, "Ach, Simon! Have you completely lost your memory! That would be Eleanor Beachy! Don't you remember her?"

Uncle Lavern was shaking his head, muttering, "Now, Joyce, you don't know that it's the same Eleanor …"

"Of course it is!" Aunt Joyce interrupted as she brushed his comment off with a wave of her hand. "Eleanor Beachy is the only Eleanor here in our community. It has to be her!" Directing her full attention on her nephew, Joyce explained, "Simon … can't you remember? When you came to visit us that last year when you were a little boy, you and Eleanor spent the entire summer playing together! You ran through the fields together and caught wild kittens … played games until the sun went down every night …"

The longer his aunt talked, the quicker the memories came back to Simon. He felt like he was being assailed by glimpses of the past.

It was the same girl! No wonder Eleanor had looked familiar when he had met her on the street—Simon had known her when they were both children.

"You were in love with that girl," Aunt Joyce concluded, "Absolutely head over heels for her. I thought that it was going to rip both of your hearts apart when you had to leave."

Nodding his head, Simon could remember those days. He had truly thought that Eleanor Beachy hung the stars with her sparkling green eyes and dark brown hair. She had a way about her that seemed to stand out from other young women. She was so sweet and yet, at the same time, possessed a sort of fierce soul that dared anyone to cross her.

Even now, Simon felt a smile start to cross his lips at the memory of their old times together. It felt like a flood from the past had suddenly assailed him, reminding him of so many good times that he had shared with the spirited girl.

"You must remember now!" Aunt Joyce laughed as she sat back in her chair and picked up the sock that she had been darning. "I can see that same old look in your eyes."

Suddenly overwhelmed by embarrassment, Simon shook his head and tried to brush off whatever "look" his aunt was referring to.

"So that's Eleanor." Simon gave it his best attempt at sounding unconcerned as he rocked back and forth in the wooden rocker. "Well, she sure has changed some over the last few years."

"Got a mighty deal prettier, if you ask me!" Aunt Joyce threw in once again. Although she was working on darning the pair of socks, Simon could see that her eyes kept traveling back to him.

"I wish I'd known who she was," Simon continued, hoping that he could get out his statement without revealing more than he wanted. "It would have been good to talk for a while … to catch up after so much time has passed us by."

"Best be leaving that one alone, nephew," Uncle Lavern spoke up, his eyes looking serious. "If you truly talked to Eleanor Beachy today, then it's best you realize that she has a beau who happens to be mighty protective of her. They've been courting for several years and, needless to say, I think he's working toward an engagement."

Just hearing the words made Simon feel like his heart had dropped down into his stomach. Swallowing hard, he thought back to the young man who had arrived when he was talking to Eleanor and had practically dragged the pretty young woman away. It wasn't hard to imagine that he might be the protective type.

"Oh, Lavern!" Joyce spoke up with irritation, shaking her head. "All Simon wants to do is catch up with her and talk some … he isn't saying anything about swooping in and snatching her away from Abe!" Rolling her eyes, she turned back toward Simon and smiled with a twinkle in her eyes. "If you want to see Eleanor again, she walks from her home on the edge of town to her father's candle shop every morning."

With that, Aunt Joyce sat back and closed her mouth, obviously not wanting to upset her husband any more than she already had.

Uncle Lavern was silent as well as he continued to read over his magazine, only shaking his head slowly in disapproval.

Simon leaned back in his own chair and mulled over his aunt's words. It felt like it was almost too much to process. What were the chances that, after all these years, he would just happen upon his childhood sweetheart and still feel such a strong connection to her? As much as he hated to admit it, Simon had almost entirely forgotten her over the years. What sense did it make that he would feel such an intense pull toward her when their hands touched out on the street?

What was he supposed to do now? Should Simon follow Aunt Joyce's suggestion that he talk to Eleanor once again, or would he be wiser to follow Uncle Lavern's warning and stay away from her?

While Simon wasn't sure which option was actually the best, he knew that he had to talk to her again.

Closing his eyes, Simon took in a deep breath. He planned to go back to that spot and wait for her the next morning. Wise or not, he couldn't let his childhood friend go without at least reintroducing himself.

Chapter Three

Standing on the corner of the street, Simon felt awkward as he tried to appear inconspicuous as he waited for Eleanor to arrive. Glancing at the time that was displayed on a large clock in front of a nearby bank, he took in a deep breath and let it out slowly. Surely he had already been waiting long enough; perhaps she was sick or had decided to take the day off of work.

Looking into a store window, Simon hoped that he wouldn't appear to be a stalker as he waited for his old childhood friend to arrive.

His eyes darting from the store front to the sidewalk, he felt his heart start beating faster when he caught sight of a black Amish bonnet headed his direction. Turning around to get a better look, Simon could see Eleanor headed right toward him; however, she was looking into the street, waving at cars that were passing her by.

Just the sight of her made it hard for Simon to breathe normally. He was almost overcome by a desire to go bounding across the sidewalk toward her and to take her in his arms, holding onto her as he admitted their past connection as children.

But, just as Simon took a step forward, he realized that Eleanor was not alone. At her side was the familiar and somewhat intimidating form of her boyfriend.

"Abe." Simon muttered the name under his breath, almost as if it was a sort of cursed word that couldn't be spoken aloud.

Gritting his teeth together, Simon watched the way that Eleanor's boyfriend grabbed onto her arm and held it tightly, almost as if she was a possession rather than a treasured sweetheart. Abe had his jaw jutted forward in defiance against the world as he stared at the passing cars, giving them a stern nod of acknowledgement.

It seemed so strange to look at the difference between Eleanor and her beau. While Eleanor seemed so carefree and friendly, it looked as if Abe Miller held a grudge against the entire world.

Seeing Eleanor's future fiancé made Simon feel almost sick to his stomach. A deep sense of jealousy infected his entire being, and he had to battle not to jump out of the shadows and punch the other man in the face.

Forcing himself to remain calm and act respectful toward Eleanor's choice, Simon turned and walked the other direction. He would try again tomorrow. Simon didn't know how long it would take, but eventually he would have a chance to talk with the girl who he used to care for so deeply.

But, despite Simon's best intentions, he would soon discover that finding a chance to talk with Eleanor was not as easy as he had initially hoped. Day after day, he would return to the street, only to find her walking arm in arm with Abe. It seemed that she was almost within reach and yet her boyfriend put a thousand-mile chasm between them.

***

Eleanor awoke to the sound of birds singing outside of her window. Glancing at the windup clock that sat next to her bed, she took in a deep breath and forced herself into a sitting position.

It was Friday.

Smiling into the empty room, Eleanor considered what that meant.

The week was almost over!

Despite the fun that Eleanor had in her father's shop, sometimes she felt exhausted and overwhelmed by the amount of work. While her father stayed home to make the candles with Eleanor's mother, she was left to go to the shop and work to display and then provide the specialty candles to their wide selection of both Amish and Englisch customers.

Pulling on her clothes and putting her prayer kapp on top of her head, Eleanor found her thoughts traveling back to Abe. Ever since Eleanor had encountered Simon Nissley, Abe had stuck by her side like glue. While Eleanor usually walked herself to work, Abe had not let her out of his sight for the past three days.

While there was something nice about his jealousy and concern, Eleanor found it almost suffocating. She wasn't married to Abe, and yet it felt like he considered her to be solely his … more like a piece of property than anything else. Sometimes, Eleanor wasn't sure if Abe actually loved her or if he just didn't want anyone else to have her. He certainly didn't do much to show any form of affection toward her.

Gritting her teeth together, Eleanor sucked in a deep breath of the chilly air. At least this morning would be different. Abe was supposed to be working with his father in a faraway town and wouldn't be available to walk her to or from work. Although Eleanor could find the trip somewhat lonely, she would actually rather be alone at times.

Shaking her head, Eleanor tried to push the terrible thought out of her mind.

How could she feel that way about Abe? Hadn't she felt like she was completely in love with him at one point? When had things changed?

No matter how she might feel, Eleanor knew that she had to keep the course and continue as planned. She knew that Abe was looking forward to an engagement, and she expected him to ask for her hand any day now. It was time for her to resign herself to her fate and stop acting like she had any options.

After courting Abe for two years, she needed to realize that he was as good as it was going to get for her.

***

Standing alongside the street, Simon felt like a complete fool. This made the fourth day that he had stood on the sidewalk, hoping to catch Eleanor by herself. Surely, this was the craziest thing that he had ever done in all of his nineteen years.

Closing his eyes, Simon breathed a quick prayer under his breath, "Gott … maybe I'm insane. I'm standing out here in the cold, waiting on a girl who doesn't remember me … who I haven't talked to since we were children. Gott, if you want me to talk to her, then you're going to have to help me. This is the last day that I'm standing out here waiting. If you want us to get to see each other, then please give me an opportunity."

Swallowing hard, Simon slowly opened his eyes. Glancing into the distance, he could see a familiar black Amish bonnet headed his way.

Squinting his eyes, Simon could see that she was alone. Feeling his heart give a leap in his chest, it felt like it was almost too good to even hope was true. Surely Abe was following along behind but simply hadn't come into view yet.

But the closer that Eleanor got, the more obvious it became that she was all by herself.

Suddenly, Simon felt like he might be sick with nerves. Forcing himself to step out of the shadows, he smiled in her direction, his mind completely going blank as he searched for the right words to say.

"Good morning!" Simon called out the first thing that came to his mind.

Eleanor raised her eyebrows and turned to look at him in surprise, her jaw dropping open as she replied, "Ach, good morning! You're Simon … right?"

She had remembered his name! Not only had she remembered his name, but Simon could detect a twinkle in her eye that came when she recognized him.

Smiling and nodding, Simon replied, "Jah … Simon … yes, that's me."

Eleanor laughed at him, her voice sounding like twinkling bells as she replied, "Well, it's good to see you again! I thought maybe you were just passing through."

Simon loved that voice—he felt like he wanted to listen to it for the rest of his life. He wanted to get lost in the cheerfulness that she presented to everyone she encountered. Shaking his head, Simon explained, "No. I'm here for a while … staying with my aunt and uncle."

Looking toward the clock at the nearby bank, Eleanor's expression seemed to sober as she admitted, "My, I'd like to chat, but I have to get on to work … my daed's candle shop is about to open for the day … and it can't open unless I'm there with the key." She laughed again as she held up the metal key.

Smiling in spite of himself, Simon suggested, "Could I maybe walk along with you? I'm headed that direction, anyway."

He felt himself holding his breath, hoping for all he was worth that the beautiful young woman would say yes. It seemed a risky thing to ask since her harsh-looking boyfriend might be hiding around any corner, for all that Simon knew, but it was a risk that he was willing to take.

A look of apprehension seemed to cross Eleanor's face before she nodded and replied, "Sure. I would like that! That would be good."

Simon walked alongside her, soaking in the opportunity to be so close to the lovely girl. Over the past few days, he had rehearsed the ways that he would tell her about the time they used to spend together as children, but now, well, now it all seemed so difficult to put into words.

"So, how long are you here for?" Eleanor interrupted his thoughts, "You said that you're visiting relatives …"

Interrupting, Simon replied, "I'm actually hoping to move into the area. I used to come here as a boy to stay with family and I just fell in love with Indiana … it's always felt like home."

Simon watched her carefully, hoping that she would begin to recognize him or that something he said would spark a memory from the past.

"Oh, I understand!" Eleanor exclaimed, her infectious smile spreading across her face. "I can't imagine living anywhere else."

Stopping in front of a shop, Eleanor reached into her pocket and pulled out the key. Smiling softly, she turned to look him in the eyes as she explained, "Well, I have to get in here to work …" Her voice seemed to trail off, and her eyes lingered on Simon.

Simon felt like this was his one opportunity to talk her and that he was blowing it completely. Looking into her eyes, Simon could almost sense that she was also upset that that their visit had to end.

Reaching out, he grabbed her hand in his own and stared into her eyes as he whispered a hoarse question. "Is there any chance that I could walk you home after you get off from work?"

A look of uncertainty crossed Eleanor's face, and her eyes seemed to cloud over. For a minute, Simon was afraid that he might have pushed too far. Ever so slowly, her head began to nod, and she softly replied, "Jah, sure. That would be nice." Her voice growing stronger, she explained, "My boyfriend usually walks me home from work, but he's not going to be here today … he's away, working in the city, and won't be back until late. So yes, it would be great to have some company."

Simon couldn't stop the grin that spread across his face. It felt like he was so happy that he couldn't contain himself. Nodding vigorously, he replied, "I'll be here. I'll see you around five!"

Walking away from the small candle shop, Simon kept turning back around and looking toward the spot where Eleanor had been standing only moments earlier.

Finally, Simon had found the chance to talk to Eleanor! While he might have not said everything that he had hoped, he could enjoy the knowledge that he would get a second opportunity that afternoon. Not only would he get the chance to spend time with Eleanor, but he now knew that her boyfriend was out of town and wouldn't be able to get upset about their visit.

Grinning from ear to ear, Simon practically bounded down the street. He suddenly felt more alive than he had in years!

Chapter Four

Standing at the counter in her father's candle shop, Eleanor reached up to rub at her eyes before glancing at the grandfather clock that was positioned against the wall. It was almost five o'clock. Grabbing for a paper, Eleanor wrote down a few notes and then stuffed them into the pocket of her dress.

She had to remember to tell her father about a special candle order and, considering the way that her brain had been working that day, it seemed unlikely that she would have the presence of mind to remember without a note.

Letting out a deep breath, Eleanor tried to keep a smile from playing at the corner of her lips. It seemed that her thoughts had continuously returned to Simon that day. His image felt like it had been engraved in her mind, and the tone of his deep voice played through her thoughts almost as clearly as if he was still by her side.

As much as Eleanor hated to admit it, she could hardly wait to see him again. She wanted desperately to talk to him and to find out more about his life.

Standing up straighter, Eleanor felt like her mind was going to drive her insane. She felt her emotions drifting from being enthusiastic about seeing Simon to being overwhelmingly guilt-ridden that she wasn't thinking more about Abe. Truth be told, Eleanor felt more attraction toward Simon than she had ever shared with Abe … and that alone made her feel terrible about herself.

The sound of a gentle rap against the door made Eleanor feel like she might be sick to her stomach. She practically jumped with mingled nerves and excitement as she hurried to unlock it and ushered Simon into the shop.

"Hello!" she exclaimed, unable to stop a smile from plastering itself across her face. "Well, it's good to see you again." Even as the words escaped her lips, Eleanor felt like they sounded stupid. As a blush began to climb across her cheeks, she explained, "I'm almost ready to go."

Simon nodded his head and began asking her about her day.

Soon, they were on the street, headed toward Eleanor's home. While Eleanor was a bundle of nerves, it seemed that conversation came increasingly easily. Simon was so pleasant to talk to, asking her questions about what had happened at the shop and sharing stories with her.

It was strange for Eleanor to have a young man that she could actually have a conversation with. Too often, it felt like Abe didn't even give her a chance to talk and when he did, he acted like the things she said were more of a nuisance than anything else. Sometimes, Abe could get irritable just hearing about the simplest things; a story about a woman picking up candles might be enough to make him snappy and angry.

Eleanor savored every minute that she spent at Simon's side, trying her best to suck in what might be her only chance to be alone with the handsome young stranger.

They were drawing near the outskirts of town when Simon turned to look at her, his dark eyes growing serious as he asked, "Eleanor … do you know my aunt and uncle? I mentioned them the other day … when we first met. Lavern and Joyce."

Eleanor nodded her head, wondering where this strange turn in conversation was going.

"I used to stay with my aunt and uncle during the summers," Simon continued, his voice sounding somewhat strained as he continued his story. "When I was here, I used to play with a little girl … a little girl named Eleanor Beachy."

As the words escaped Simon's lips, Eleanor felt her heart give a leap inside her chest. Suddenly, recognition hit her. Stopping dead in her tracks, Eleanor stared straight into Simon's eyes.

"You're not … you're …" Eleanor felt like she couldn't even get the words to come out of her mouth without stuttering. "Are you really that Simon?"

Simon was smiling now, nodding his head as his own cheeks seemed to grow red.

"That would be me," Simon returned, "I'm the Simon who used to play with you."

"Wow," Eleanor breathed softly as a lump seemed to collect in her throat. "I can't believe…you've changed." She grimaced as she heard what she had said. Yes, it was true … Simon had changed. He had gone from a rough and rowdy little boy to a handsome man.

"I mean, I would have never recognized you," she continued, hoping that he couldn't read her thoughts.

Simon smiled and nodded his head, "You've grown up a lot yourself."

Thinking back to their childhood days, Eleanor admitted, "I never thought I would see you again. You came for the summer, and then you were gone." Lowering her voice, she whispered the truth into the wind, "I was only eleven, but I was heartbroken to lose you."

Simon reached out and took his hand in his own, looking down into her eyes with a gaze that spoke so many words. In that minute, Eleanor felt like she was finally where she was supposed to be. Standing there next to Simon, with the feel of his strong hand holding onto hers, surely this was what she had waited for all of these years!

"Eleanor!"

A harsh voice interrupted their special moment together and Eleanor felt a sudden burst of nausea hit her.

Turning around, she could see that Abe was headed her direction. She had been so sure that he would be away until late tonight, but here he was, marching toward her with his jaw clenched and his hands balled up into fists.

Looking up into Simon's face, Eleanor could see that his own jaw was working as he tried to hold in his emotions. He seemed to be totally disgusted that Abe was ruining their time together, and Eleanor was afraid that he might decide to do something harsh such as confront Abe.

"Ach, Simon," Eleanor whispered, hoping to defuse whatever was about to happen. "That's my boyfriend. I've got to go. I am so sorry, but I have to go."

Jerking away from Simon's gentle hold on her hand, Eleanor turned to meet her boyfriend.

"Abe!" she exclaimed, trying to stop her trembling voice as her boyfriend reached her side. Looking at Abe, she could see that his face was sullen and he eyed her suspiciously as he reached out and grabbed onto her arm.

"Eleanor!" he snarled in a voice that was even harsher than usual, "What are you doing out here … and with him?"

He turned and gave Simon a dirty stare, his eyes narrowing even more as if he was sizing the other man up.

"I'm sorry, Abe," Eleanor hurried to explain. "This is my old friend, Simon. We used to know each other when we were children. We were just talking about the old days."

"Let's just get you home," Abe continued as he tightened his grip on Eleanor's arm and jerked her toward her house, leaving Simon behind.

Simon watched as Eleanor was practically dragged down the street by her boyfriend. The feelings of irritation that had been simmering in Simon's heart suddenly reached a boiling point. It took everything within him not to rush forward and punch the other man in the stomach.

How was it possible for Abe to have such a wonderful girlfriend and yet to treat her so viciously?

Realizing that his best and only option was to simply leave, Simon forced himself to turn around and walk back toward Uncle Lavern's house.

Simon felt like his emotions were in a blender as he considered all that had happened over the last twelve hours. He had finally had the opportunity to talk with Eleanor and, to his surprise, she had seemed to actually want to talk to him. Surely he hadn't just imagined the look that he'd seen in her eyes—a soft look that made him feel like she wished that they could spend more time together. And when Simon had reminded her about their time together, it had been obvious that Eleanor was happy to be reunited.

But then, just as things had been going well, Abe had appeared and ruined it all.

As he reached Uncle Lavern's house, Simon pushed the door open and stepped inside where Aunt Joyce was busy setting plates around the table.

"Simon!" she exclaimed as he stepped inside. "You certainly took your time getting home! Where have you been?"

Pulling out a chair at the table, Simon took in a deep breath as he sat down in one of the seats and let out a deep sigh. "I've been on a walk."

"A walk?" Aunt Joyce repeated as she scooped some baked chicken onto a plate and set it on the table. "Where were you walking to?"

Simon tried to decide how much he should share with his aunt. Uncle Lavern suddenly appeared from a back room and sat down at the table across from Simon. "Evening, Simon." His uncle gave a stiff smile as he reached for the butter dish and began to spread some out on his plate beside a homemade biscuit.

"So, where did you walk?" Aunt Joyce repeated. That was Aunt Joyce … never one to give up when she saw an opportunity to hear some interesting news.

Letting out a deep breath, Simon admitted, "I ended up walking Eleanor Beachy home."

Aunt Joyce clapped her chubby hands together and sat down across from him with a grin spread across her round face. "Oh my! So you finally got to talk to her?"

"Joyce," Uncle Lavern scolded gently. "Let the boy have some privacy!"

Ignoring her husband entirely, Joyce leaned forward so that she was closer to Simon and stared at him intently. "What happened?"

Swallowing hard around the lump that was forming in his throat, Simon looked at the food spread out on the table and thought that he might be sick. The idea of eating was almost more than he could stand and yet, at the same time, he knew that he would have to force some down or else risk even more questions from his aunt.

"Well," he admitted slowly, "I met her on the way to work and then offered to walk her home this afternoon. We walked back toward her house … and I told her how we used to be friends."

Glancing up at Joyce, Simon could see that his aunt was now fairly beaming and listening almost as intently as if she was hearing a story straight out of a book.

"Things seemed to be going well …" Simon tried to shorten his story so that things wouldn't be as awkward as they felt. "She remembered me, and we had a nice conversation. Then her boyfriend showed up, and I came home."

"Her boyfriend showed up?" Aunt Joyce's face fell and her brows knit together in a frown. "Abe? How dare he show up at a moment like that!"

"Joyce," Uncle Lavern reached out to put a steadying hand on her arm. "Leave the boy be. This isn't our battle to get involved in. Eleanor Beachy and Abe Miller have been a couple for years now. It's time to just let this go."

Aunt Joyce seemed to pay attention to his words and shut her mouth. Motioning that it was time to pray, Uncle Lavern led the family through the silent blessing.

While Simon was trying to pray, it felt like any words that came to mind kept getting blocked as images of Abe crossed through his mind.

As soon as Uncle Lavern said "amen," the family began passing around the delicious food. Even though he had no appetite, Simon forced himself to dish large helpings of green bean casserole, baked chicken, mashed potatoes, and noodles onto his plate.

"What do you all know about Abe?" Simon asked, unable to keep the question to himself any longer.

Both Aunt Joyce and Uncle Lavern looked up in surprise before glancing at each other.

"Well," Aunt Joyce started slowly as she cut her biscuit in half and began to spread butter across the flaky bread. "He's been in our community for about two and a half years now. No one really knew him or his family before they moved here from Pennsylvania. His family seems like they're good people … but Abe is the baby of the family and a bit spoiled."

Even Uncle Lavern was nodding his head at

her correct pronouncement, tossing in his own word of explanation. "Abe is a fiery one, to be sure. But his bark seems a lot worse than his bite. I don't think that he's ever been really mean to Eleanor as far as anyone can tell …"

"But she's not happy with him." Aunt Joyce added.

"How can you tell that?" Simon asked as he made himself take a bite of chicken.

"I can tell these things," Joyce replied, turning to look at her own meal. "I always had hoped that someday you'd be able to come back and pick up where you left off with Eleanor. But it seemed that Abe beat you to it. I wouldn't be so upset if I actually thought that she was happy with him, but she just seems more resigned than anything else."

The idea of Eleanor simply being resigned to her fate was almost more than Simon could stand. Gritting his teeth together, he tried to determine what he would do next.

Taking in a deep breath, he asked, "Aunt Joyce … do they still have the young people's singings on Sunday night?"

Smiling, Joyce replied, "Why, of course they do."

Nodding his head resolutely, Simon announced, "Well, I plan to be there this Sunday night. Seems if I am going to live here, I might as well get involved in the community."

Simon could see that his aunt was thrilled with his proclamation. The wide grin that spread across her face gave him courage, and he could feel the smile that he had worn earlier returning to his own lips.

Chapter Five

Sunday morning, Eleanor felt like her heart was in her throat as she sat through church beside her mother. Try as she might to keep her eyes to herself, she couldn't keep her gaze from returning to Simon as he sat on the other side of the building. There was something about him that seemed to simply magnetize her to him. It was so hard to believe that he was the same boy that she had loved as a girl and yet, at the same time, so easy to imagine.

Shaking her head, Eleanor tried to force her mind to remain on the sermon that was being delivered by Preacher Jake.

Eleanor could remember a time when she had told her friends that she would marry

Simon one day. Words that had been spoken with such sincerity and yet forgotten so quickly.

Glancing down at her hands, Eleanor considered all that had happened in her life since those childhood dreams. She had grown up and met Abe … and thoughts of Simon had long been tossed aside.

I wonder what my life would be like if I had not accepted Abe's proposal to court? Eleanor questioned herself. I wonder what life would be like if Simon had come to town while I was still single?

Even as the thought pushed its way through her mind, Eleanor felt a stab of guilt overtake her. How could she even be thinking such things? Surely thinking about Simon was evil after all that had happened between her and Abe!

Suddenly, Eleanor realized that the sermon was over. Pulling herself to her feet, she followed her parents out of the house where church had been held and toward their waiting buggy. A part of her wanted desperately for Simon to come chasing after her, while another part of her held her breath, hoping that she wouldn't face him at all.

"Eleanor." It was the voice of Abe that stopped her when she was almost to her parents' buggy. "Eleanor, would you be willing to let me take you home?"

Eleanor couldn't hide the fact that she had been more than a little put out with her boyfriend ever since he'd rudely interrupted her conversation with Simon on Friday night.

He had been harsh to her that night, going so far as to almost bruise her arm as he had dragged her to the house.

Deciding that her best option was to simply make up with him and hope for better times ahead, Eleanor nodded her head slowly. "Jah, Abe. Sure."

The ride to Eleanor's house was silent for the most part. It seemed so hard for her to find the words to speak to her boyfriend after he had made her so mad the previous Friday.

Finally, Abe was the one to break the silence as he guided his horse down the road.

"Eleanor," he spoke up with a sigh, "I know that you're mad at me. I know that I made you angry on Friday night when I interrupted your visit with that guy …"

Bristling, Eleanor sat up straighter in her seat and pulled farther away from Abe. "You made me angry because you were so rude … and it felt like you were going to break my arm in two dragging me around like I was a stray dog rather than your girlfriend."

Out of the corner of her eye, Eleanor could see Abe roll his eyes before announcing, "Good grief, it wasn't that bad!" Softening some, he went on to explain, "Eleanor, I'm sorry. I know that it's hard for you to understand, but I love you. That's why I get so rough with you at times. I love you so much that the idea of someone else taking you … well, it makes me terribly upset. I hate the thought of anything ever getting between us."

As Abe spoke, Eleanor couldn't decide if she felt sorry for him or if she'd rather slap him in the face. No matter how she might feel, she knew that it would be best to simply end the fight. Gathering all her courage, she muttered the words that she hated to say, "I'm sorry, Abe."

Somehow, the apology felt dirty as it came off of her lips. She wasn't sure why she should be the one saying that she was sorry when he was the one who had been rude and had hurt her. That seemed to be the way that things had always gone, though—whenever Abe did something that was hurtful or cruel, he expected Eleanor to apologize to him.

For a moment, Eleanor wished that she could take her apology back and truly give him a piece of her mind. She wished that she could simply tell him that things were over and be done with the relationship once and for all. But how could she do that? Even though she was disgusted with Abe, he was her first beau.

First beau other than Simon, she thought to herself.

Forcing Simon out of her mind, Eleanor tried to focus on more pleasant topics.

"Are you going to be taking me to the singing tonight?" Eleanor asked.

Shaking his head, Abe rolled his eyes once again as he huffed out, "Have you forgotten? I'm supposed to go visit my grandmother this afternoon! For pity's sake, Eleanor … I told you that days ago! Don't you have anything in your head?"

Narrowing her eyes, Eleanor balled her hands up into fists.

"You can come along with me to Grandmother's house, if you want, I suppose," Abe announced, almost as if she would be more a nuisance than anything else.

Shaking her head, Eleanor replied, "No, thank you. I think I'll pass."

Eleanor would be staying behind so that she could go to the singing. And, although she didn't want to admit it even to herself, she certainly hoped that Simon Nissley would be there!

***

Simon pulled his buggy up to the Jacobson house where the young people's singing was taking place. Although it was just getting dark, it seemed like the small yard was already full of Amish teenagers enjoying their chance to socialize.

Putting his horse in the barn where it would be shielded from the chilly night air,

Simon found himself hoping once again that Eleanor would be here.

Shaking his head, Simon realized that the thought alone was ridiculous. Of course Eleanor would probably be here, but it was a sure thing that Abe would be at her side … protecting her from anyone who might try to talk to her.

Making his way to the house, Simon began to wonder if he had made a mistake coming at all. Wasn't he just torturing himself by going to see her when she already had a boyfriend?

Urging himself forward, Simon decided that even seeing a glimpse of Eleanor would be worth the torture.

Stepping into the warmth of the Jacobson house, Simon soaked up the heat from the coal stove. Pulling off his coat and putting it aside on the back of a chair, Simon made his way through the throng of Amish young folk.

"Hello there!"

The voice was so cheerful and bright that Simon felt like his heart was going to stop beating. Surely that couldn't truly be Eleanor! Why would she be talking to him? If it was really her, she would be off spending time with her boyfriend. Turning around, Simon could hardly believe his eyes when he saw that it really was the beautiful young woman from his past, standing behind him.

"Eleanor." His voice almost trembled as he spoke her name. Looking around, he was afraid that he might catch sight of Abe coming to spoil the moment completely.

Almost as if she could read his thoughts, Eleanor interrupted to say, "Abe isn't here tonight. He had to go away to see his grandmother."

As Simon watched her, he could almost sense the apprehension she was feeling as she looked down at her black shoes and clasped her hands behind her back.

"If you'd like, we could finish our conversation before the music starts," she suggested.

Nodding his head, Simon felt his face break out into another big grin as he followed her to a couple of chairs sitting apart from the rest of the group. It was beginning to look like there truly was hope for him to get to know Eleanor. and he thanked Gott for every minute they spent together.

For the next few hours, Simon and Eleanor were inseparable. It felt as if they had turned back the hands of time and were as close friends as if they had never been parted. They spent their night talking together and then, when the singing started, they gathered around the table to sing the familiar songs and hymns with the others in the Amish community.

Once they had finished their meal and everyone was done visiting, some of the young people started to leave.

Gathering all his courage, Simon asked, "Since Abe isn't here, would ya like a ride home in my buggy?"
Eleanor's face blushed red and she seemed to look around to see who was watching before she nodded her head and smiled. "Sure. That would be great!"

Seated up on the buggy with Eleanor at his side, Simon felt like he could hardly hold in his excitement. Although the night was chilly, he was so happy that he hardly noticed.

"So," Eleanor started slowly as Simon led his horse down the road, "I guess you already know that Abe and I have been going out together for years now."

Just the mention of Abe made Simon sober. He hated thinking about Eleanor's boyfriend and wished that he could forget that the other man even existed.

Clucking his tongue to urge the horses to trot a bit faster, Simon solemnly asked, "Do you love him?"

Eleanor seemed to choose her words carefully as she explained, "I'm not sure. I'm not really sure at all. It seems so wrong to say no! Abe and I have been a couple for all my courting years. He's got his good points. Sometimes, I'm not really sure about anything at all …"

As her voice trailed off, Simon couldn't stop himself. Reaching out to bridge the distance between them, he took her small, soft hand in his own and whispered, "Eleanor … I understand that you've already got a beau. I understand that I've not been a part of your life for many years. But, despite all the time that's passed between us, there's still a special place for you in my heart."
In the light of the moon, Simon thought that he could see tears glistening in Eleanor's eyes. She was quiet for a minute before announcing, "And there's a special place for you in mine as well. But, as much as I'd like for things to work out between us, the truth

remains that I just don't know how they ever can. Abe and I have been together for so long … well, I'd feel almost sinful to leave him now."

Nodding his head, Simon tried to accept this miserable announcement. It felt like his dreams had been dashed just as quickly as they had started to come true.

"I understand that," Simon replied as calmly as he could, "I understand that you've already got a life planned with someone else. But I want you to know that, if anything changes, I'll be here for you. I really want you to be a part of my time here."
Out of the corner of his eye, Simon could see Eleanor smile, and she squeezed his hand tighter against her own.

Chapter Six

Walking to her father's shop on Monday morning, Eleanor found herself hoping that Abe would decide not to meet her on her journey. It seemed that he went through waves of wanting to be with her and then times that he would rather spend his energy on someone else. Eleanor could only hope that this day, he would leave her in peace.

As embarrassed as Eleanor was to admit it, it felt like her brain was in a blender where her entire romantic situation was concerned. On one hand, she had the memory of the previous evening that she had spent with Simon. There certainly was a kind of chemistry between them that was indescribable. It felt like she and Simon were the same type of person simply placed in different bodies. He was like a piece of her heart that she hadn't known was missing.

But, on the other hand, there was Abe. Eleanor had gone out with Abe for two years. She couldn't feel that she truly cared for him, but it just seemed so wrong to leave him after they had such a history between them. He had come to depend on her to be there for him, and Eleanor couldn't stand to let him down now.

Reaching up to adjust a strand of loose hair under her prayer kapp, Eleanor shook her head.

If only she could know what Gott wanted for her life!

"Please, Gott!" Eleanor spoke into the morning air. "Give me some direction. Let me know what you want for my life."

As Eleanor stepped onto the sidewalk, she felt her stomach lurch when she noticed the young man walking right toward her.

Abe.

He was practically marching in her direction, his face looking none too happy to see her.

Lifting a hand, Eleanor tried to wave.

"Morning!" she called out when her boyfriend drew closer.

"Eleanor." Abe spoke her name sharply without even attempting to return her greeting. "I'd like an explanation about last night."

Eleanor felt her stomach drop and a sense of fear spread through her entire body. She was used to Abe getting upset but rarely had she seen such a fire burning in his blue eyes.

"What?" she started to ask, but Abe reached out and grabbed her arm, twisting it with such force that it made her stop.

"What were you doing with that new guy?" Abe asked between gritted teeth as he squeezed harder against her arm. "What were you thinking? You're my girl! Do you hear me? Mine and no one else's!"

"Let go of me, Abe!" Eleanor exclaimed as she tried to jerk away from him, stepping backwards as her arm was set free from his grip. "I might be your girlfriend, but I'm not your property. And, considering the way that you treat me, I don't think that I want to be your girlfriend much longer either!"

Abe let out something that sounded like a low growl. He made another lunge for Eleanor, but she jumped out of the way.

Completely misstepping, Abe fell off the sidewalk and down into the road. When his body hit the pavement, he began to cry out in pain.

Eleanor felt her heart stop as she hurried to his side. Dropping down on the ground next to him, she reached out to take his dark head of hair in her hands.

"Abe!" she exclaimed, tears filling her eyes as she watched her boyfriend writhing in pain. "Abe, what's hurt?"

"My ankle!" Abe groaned as he wrapped his hand around his leg, tears beginning to stream down his cheeks. "I think it's broken. Oh, it hurts so bad!"

Standing, Eleanor motioned for an approaching car to come their direction. Suddenly, all thoughts about Simon were stripped from her mind as she explained to the driver that her boyfriend needed a ride to the hospital. At that moment, she wasn't worried about anything other than making sure that Abe got the help that he needed.

***

Sitting in the waiting room at the hospital, Eleanor felt the tears start to stream down her cheeks. Abe had been rushed back into the ER, leaving Eleanor to sit by herself. Reaching her shaking hands up to her face, she ran her fingers over her eyes, trying to wipe away the tears that were quickly starting to overtake her.

"Abe," she whispered into the stillness of the hospital room. "Abe, how could I have done this to you?"

Remembering the prayer that she had prayed, Eleanor had to feel like this was Gott's way of showing her how much she was needed in Abe's life.

The hospital doors swung open to reveal an elderly Amish couple entering the building.

Recognizing Abe's parents, Eleanor pulled herself to her feet and waited on them to come to her side.

"Eleanor!" Abe's mother cried out as she reached out and took Eleanor into her arms in a hug. "What happened? Is he going to be okay?"

Shaking her head, Eleanor explained, "He's hurt his ankle. He thought that he might have broken it, but the doctors are taking x-rays now."

"What happened?" Abe's mother pressed again.

Looking down at her shoes, Eleanor felt a sense of overpowering guilt attack her as she admitted, "He and I were arguing … and he got upset … he just fell into the street."

Glancing back up at the older woman's face, Eleanor could see a judgmental set to her jaw as she shook her head and muttered, "Tsk, tsk, tsk. Eleanor, you know how high-strung Abe can be! Why on earth were you arguing with him out in the street? Didn't you think that it might be best to just appease him by doing what he said? If only you hadn't provoked him, then this wouldn't have happened!"

Swallowing hard, Eleanor considered defending herself, but then brushed that thought away. Nodding her head slowly, she whispered, "You're probably right." Letting her voice grow stronger, she spoke out to announce, "I am going to make this right! I'll do whatever it takes to nurse Abe back to health."

The arrival of the doctor alerted them that the examination was over. Stepping up next to them, the Englisch doctor explained, "His leg isn't broken, but it's badly twisted and sprained. I don't think he can put any weight on it for at least a week. He'll need some special care …"

Before the doctor could say anything else, Eleanor was raising her hand.

"I'll do it!" she explained. "I'll do whatever it takes. I'll do whatever needs to be done to make my boyfriend well again."

And Eleanor meant what she was saying. She intended to do everything within her power to help her boyfriend recover from the injury that she had inflicted on him.

***

Sitting by the fireplace in Uncle Lavern's home, Simon had never felt any lower. After such a good weekend, it seemed that everything had fallen apart. He had received news early that week that Abe Miller had fallen during an argument with Eleanor and had badly hurt his ankle. Then Simon had heard through the Amish grapevine that

Eleanor had basically moved in with Abe's family so that she could nurse him back to health.

There was even some talk about a rumor that Eleanor would soon be engaged.

Reaching up to wipe at his eyes, Simon could only hope that his aunt and uncle wouldn't notice the tears that were begging an escape.

"I hear that Abe's getting better slowly," Uncle Lavern announced as he hammered a new nail in the wall and then rehung a calendar that had fallen earlier that day.

"Humph!" Aunt Joyce snorted as she swept some dirt up into a dustpan and then tossed it into a nearby trash can. "I have a hard time feeling too sorry for that boy. If it was possible, I would almost think that he hurt his foot on purpose, just so that Eleanor would have to nurse him back to health." Uncle Lavern let out a deep sigh and muttered, "I'm sure he didn't do that, Joyce."

"I didn't say that he did!" Joyce returned hotly. "I said that he would have if he'd thought of it!"

Simon let out a breath that was shakier than he had hoped. Looking down at his hands, he muttered, "It seems like things just fell apart right when they were starting to come together. I had finally had a chance to spend some time with Eleanor … and then this happened to pull us completely apart."

The entire room seemed to sober. Looking up, Simon saw his aunt nodding her head sympathetically, and she admitted, "I'm afraid I don't know what to say, Simon. I never should have suggested that you try to talk to her. Your uncle was right … it would have been better for you to stay out of it completely. I had just been so hopeful that things would work out between the two of you. Even when you were children, it just seemed like a match made in heaven!"

Uncle Lavern made his way across the room and sat down in one of the seats across from Simon. Sucking in a deep breath, he let it out slowly as he announced, "I think that we sometimes forget a very important fact in the midst of all our finagling and trying to make things turn out our way. Gott is still in control … and Gott needs to be in control. He is the only one who knows what is best in this situation. Maybe it's time for us to just step back and start praying that Eleanor will make the right decision." Glancing to look up at Simon, he continued, "You let her know that you like her … so you've done your part. Now, it may be time for Gott to fight for you." A smile started to spread across Lavern's face as he continued, "Of course, with Abe hurt, this would seem like a good time for you to attack him while you have the upper hand … but I don't think that would turn out well in the end."

Simon smiled softly and nodded his head. Leaning back in his seat, he closed his eyes and considered Uncle Lavern's words. It was true. He had done everything possible and it seemed like the doors were simply shutting in his face. Now that Abe was hurt, anything that Simon did to fight for Eleanor would probably work in the opposite direction—pushing her even farther away from him and closer to Abe.

But, despite all that he was up against, Simon could cling to the fact that Gott was still in control. While Simon might not know how to best handle this situation, Gott did.

But what if Gott wants Eleanor to be with Abe?

The thought almost made Simon sick to his stomach. And yet, at the same time, he realized that he was going to have to give up the girl that he loved if that was a part of Gott's plan.

"Gott," Simon whispered silently, "Please direct Eleanor. If you want her to stay with Abe, then bless their relationship. But, if you don't want things to work out between them, please open her eyes to the truth about him. Amen."

Giving it up to Gott was difficult, but Simon knew that he had to either go crazy or else give this situation up to the only One who could truly make things right.

As much as he hated to admit it, Simon was beginning to wonder if he could stand to stay in Indiana if Eleanor and Abe got married. It might be time for him to go back home to his family. It might be time for Simon to leave behind the memories of the past and instead forge a new future.

Chapter Seven

Eleanor felt totally exhausted. It was now Saturday and the week had crept by like a box turtle crawling on the road. She had been staying at Abe's house ever since the accident, spending all of her time tending to her boyfriend's needs.

With his ankle injured, Abe seemed to think that he was unable to do anything for himself. In an attempt to help him, Eleanor had had to take on a heavy load, helping him whenever he needed to get up. Her back was aching, and Eleanor was beginning to wonder if she could stand another night sitting in the hard-backed chair beside his bed with no hope of getting any sleep.

The ringing of a bedside bell alerted Eleanor that her services were needed once again. Whenever she would start to doze off or would attempt to read a book, Abe would ring the bell to let her know that he needed something else.

Pulling herself to her feet, Eleanor walked over to her boyfriend's bedside, "What do you need?"

Rolling his eyes, Abe gritted his teeth together irritably and exclaimed, "You've been here with me for six days now, Eleanor! What do you think I want?"

Eleanor searched her mind, trying to decide what it could possibly be. Shrugging, she asked, "Something to eat?"

Abe jutted out his bottom jaw and stared at her with an icy glare before snapping, "I just ate an hour ago! For goodness' sake, are you trying to fatten me up? I'm already putting on enough weight. Don't you want me to look good?"

Throwing suggestions out as they came to her mind, Eleanor asked, "Would you like to play a game of checkers? Perhaps I could read some to you from the Bible?"

Now Abe certainly scoffed, "Yeah, right! That sounds just like what I need. I'm thirsty, Eleanor! Thirsty. How would a game or some Bible reading help me with that?"

Each sharp comment hurt Eleanor a little bit more and, at the same time, seemed to get under her skin and make her even more annoyed than ever.

Sucking in a deep breath of air, Eleanor took his glass and hurried to get some well water out of a pitcher on the sink. Returning to the room, Eleanor could see that Abe still had a disgusted grimace on his face.

Taking a drink of the water, he scowled before setting the glass aside and announcing, "I hope you're happy with all of this."

Raising an eyebrow, Eleanor sat down next to his bed. "I don't know what you mean," she replied, almost afraid to try to answer one way or another. It would be a lie to say that she was happy with the situation but, at the same time, she was afraid that saying she wasn't happy would trigger some sort of temper tantrum from her boyfriend.

"Yes, happy." Abe returned, "Happy that I'm stuck here in this bed."

"Of course I'm not happy about that," Eleanor returned slowly as she leaned back in her seat, "I never would want you to be hurt."

"Humph," Abe snorted as he glanced out the window.

Watching her boyfriend, Eleanor couldn't help but wonder how hurt he actually was and how much of this event had simply turned into a show. Even as the thought crossed her mind, she had to push it away.

"If you don't like this, then you shouldn't have hurt me." Abe spoke so softly that Eleanor could hardly hear him, but at the same time, she managed to catch every word.

Her eyes getting bigger, Eleanor sat up straighter and asked, "What do you mean? I shouldn't have hurt you?"

Turning to stare her straight in the face, Abe

returned, "If you're not happy, then you shouldn't have done this. You did this, Eleanor. You. You're the reason that I'm hurt."

Opening her mouth wide, Eleanor could hardly believe what she was hearing.

Fighting the urge to laugh in amazement, Eleanor exclaimed, "You hurt yourself. You got hurt when you lunged at me and tried to grab my arm. Can't you remember our fight, Abe?"

Nodding his head, Abe grew even more sullen as he exclaimed, "Of course I remember. I remember everything about it. If you hadn't jerked away from me, then I wouldn't be lying in this bed."

Amazed at his ludicrous words, Eleanor shook her head and said, "But you were trying to hurt me! I already have bruises all over my arm!"

"Then you shouldn't have made me that mad. You know you did wrong. You did wrong when you spent time with that Simon Nissley, and you did wrong to fight with me. You were in the wrong, Eleanor."

As Eleanor listened to her boyfriend babble, she felt like her eyes had been opened. What was she doing? Why on earth was she sitting here day after day, working to nurse to health a man who wasn't even hurt? A man who had hurt himself because he was trying to attack her? The more that Eleanor considered her situation, the more ridiculous it seemed.

Suddenly, she began to see things in a different light. She had asked for Gott to show her what to do. When Abe was hurt, she'd instantly taken it to mean that she was meant to be with Abe, but now she realized that Gott had simply used the accident to show her the true colors of her boyfriend.

How could she have been so blind for so long?

"This is your fault," Abe was insisting, his voice growing more accusing by the moment. "It is your fault that I'm in this bed. I want you to apologize."

"What?" Eleanor could hardly believe what she had heard.

"I want you to get down on this floor and beg for my forgiveness," Abe finished, crossing his arms against his chest.

Suddenly, Eleanor could hold her emotions in no longer. She began to laugh. At first, it started out as a chuckle, but the longer that she laughed, the louder it grew.

Fighting to calm herself, Eleanor looked into the stunned face of her boyfriend and announced, "Abe…the only thing I can apologize for is allowing you to treat me like this for so long." Pulling herself to her feet, she tossed aside a book that she had been holding in her hands. "Take care of yourself, Abe. We're over."

Abe was speechless. Rather than speak, he just lay in bed, his eyes wide and his mouth hanging open.

Turning on her heel, Eleanor marched out of the room and then out of the house.

For the first time in two years, she felt like she had been freed from the oppression that she had endured with Abe. Like a bird let out of a cage, she felt like she might be able to fly as she made her way down the road back toward her own home.

***

Sunday night came, and Simon decided that he would skip the singing all together. The idea of going back to spend time among the other young folk was simply too painful. He had had such fun with Eleanor the week before that the thought of going and sitting alone was just too depressing.

With each day that went by, it became more obvious that he had no hope of a future with the beautiful young woman from his past. It was time for him to resign himself to the truth: Eleanor Beachy was to be Abe's wife.

Simon didn't even pay any attention when there was a knock on the door; instead, he waited on Aunt Joyce to see who was there.

When the knocking continued, Simon pulled himself to his feet, "Aunt Joyce!" he called out. "I think someone's at the door."

With no reply from Joyce or Lavern, Simon remembered that they had made a quick run into town to pick up something at the store. Letting out a deep sigh, he forced himself to walk to the door. He had no desire to see anyone, but he knew that he couldn't leave guests standing out on the porch.

Swinging the door open, Simon had to blink his eyes twice to believe who was standing in front of him.

There was Eleanor herself.

A smile on her lips and a bright blush creeping up her cheeks, Eleanor looked as pretty as a picture.

"Simon," she whispered his name softly.

"Eleanor," he returned the greeting, trying to find words to even speak. "What are you doing here?"

Stepping into the warmth of Uncle Lavern's house, Eleanor looked bashful as she glanced down at the floor.

"Simon," she said his name once again, but this time it was stronger. "Simon, things have … well, they've changed. Abe … well, I know it sounds crazy, but I have to feel like Gott opened my eyes where he is concerned. He really showed his true colors yesterday. I know that he's not the man for me."

Simon felt his heart give a leap in his chest. He didn't know how to accept the words that she was saying to him.

Reaching out slowly, Eleanor put a hand on his arm and continued, "Simon, you told me last week that, if anything ever changed, you would be here for me." Looking up to meet his eyes with a tender gaze of her own, she said, "Things have changed for sure. I don't know what can happen between us, Simon … but I am certain that I want to get to know you better. I want you to be a part of my life. Will you still let me learn about you? Can we get reacquainted?"

Simon could hold in his emotions no longer. He found himself battling tears as he reached out and took the beautiful young woman's hands in his own. Smiling into her face, he explained, "I know that we can't take things too fast, but I'm willing to wait, Eleanor. I'll do whatever it takes to keep you in my life."

Eleanor smiled back at him and squeezed his hands tightly.

Motioning toward the fire, Simon suggested, "Would ya like to sit down for a bit? Maybe we can get reacquainted over a bowl of popcorn."

A beautiful grin spread across Eleanor's face and she nodded her head. "Jah, that would be great!"

Leading Eleanor over to the fire, Simon felt like his heart was so full that he could contain it no longer. He didn't know what the future held, but he knew this much—with Eleanor by his side and Gott in his heart, Simon was ready for whatever it might bring.

***

Sitting across from Simon, Eleanor felt like she was soaking up every word between them. There was something about him that just seemed magnetic. She couldn't help but compare how she'd felt around Abe to the way that she felt when she was spending time with Simon.

With Abe, it had seemed that she was constantly walking on eggshells, worried that one wrong word might make him crack and say or do something harsh. She considered all the times that she had found herself watching every word she spoke, afraid that it might unleash a barrage of insults and physical harm.

But, talking with Simon, it seemed like everything came so easily. He was so laid-back and anxious to hear what she had to say and tell her things about himself.

"Thank you, Gott," Eleanor whispered as she found herself staring at her handsome childhood friend. She wished that she could somehow freeze this moment and save it in her mind to revisit later.

For so many years, Eleanor had dreamed of adventure and excitement. She had watched the train with a sort of longing in her heart, wishing that she could follow it wherever it led. She had dated Abe only because he'd fallen into her lap, but she had never been happy.

In this moment, Eleanor realized that she wouldn't change her life for anything. She was exactly where Gott wanted her to be, and she felt that she was happier than she ever could have imagined possible.

Eleanor didn't know how long it would take for her to get to know Simon or if their relationship would even progress beyond friendship, but she knew that she was anxious for anything that might come their way.

Epilogue

Eleanor stood by the kitchen window and looked out across the backyard. Watching her little daughter, Claire, playing with one of the neighbor boys, she smiled softly to herself. The children's antics kept her entertained, for sure. So entertained that she often found it difficult to get her chores done around the house.

Reaching down to pat her round stomach, Eleanor whispered, "You're slowing me down a bit too, little one!"

There was something about knowing that she had a baby growing inside of her that always made Eleanor so happy, although it certainly made it harder for her to get around and do her chores.

Of course, even when it was difficult to get everything done, she always had her sweet husband to help her around the house. Simon was a blessing, for sure, in every way possible. Even when he was tired to the bone from helping his Uncle Lavern in the woodworking shop, he would happily come home and help out with the household chores.

"What are you doing?"

Simon's voice alerted Eleanor that her husband had already arrived home from work and had managed to sneak into the house without her knowing it.

He stepped up closer to her and put his arms around her, pulling her close against him.

"Ach," Eleanor laughed as she let her body melt into his. "I was just thinking about my wonderful husband … wondering when he'd be home."

Grinning from ear to ear, Simon announced, "Well, here I am, you lucky girl!"

Standing on tiptoe, Eleanor gave him a peck on the lips before she motioned toward the window, "Look out there at those two, will ya?"

Stepping up next to her, Simon looked out the window and let out a whistle. "Those two sure are as thick as thieves, aren't they?"

Nodding her head, Eleanor smiled. "Jah. I think our little Claire may have already found herself a beau … even though she is only six years old."

Laughing, Simon gave her a knowing look as he announced, "That doesn't always turn out so bad, does it?"

Shaking her head, Eleanor leaned closer against him and looked up lovingly into his face. "No, it certainly does not."

As her husband embraced her, Eleanor had to consider how blessed she truly was. Gott had been working in her life in a mighty way, bringing a good man into her path even when she was just a child. And how happy she was that He had given her so many good things!

The End

More Amish Romance

Amish Tears

Amish Rebellion

Amish Heartbreak

Amish Secrets

Amish Questions

Amish Christmas Hope

Made in the USA
Middletown, DE
05 March 2019